THE DAY SIDNEY WAS LOST

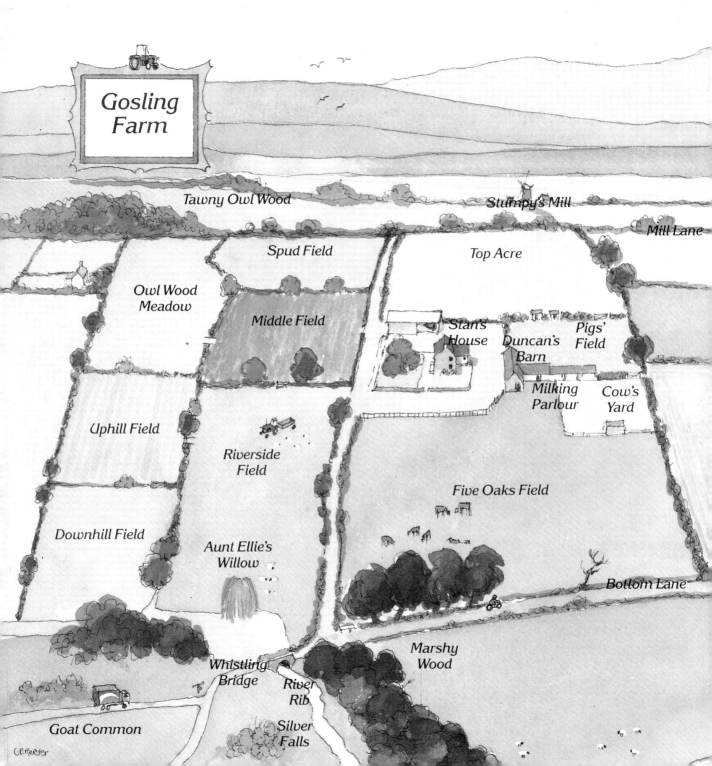

Wrigglesworth

Beech Farm

Walter's Garage

Heronwood Lake

River Dean

For Kerrie

First published by William Collins Sons & Co Ltd 1990
First published in Picture Lions 1992

Picture Lions is an imprint of the Children's Division,
part of HarperCollins Publishers Limited,
77-85 Fulham Palace Road, Hammersmith,
London W6 8JB

Cover design by Claire Jones
Printed in Great Britain by
BPCC Hazell Books, Paulton and Aylesbury

A LITTLE RED TRACTOR BOOK

THE DAY SIDNEY WAS LOST

COLIN REEDER

Text by Elizabeth Laird

PictureLions

An Imprint of HarperCollins*Publishers*

It was hot in the yard at Gosling Farm. The swallows darted in and out of the barn with food for their babies. The sun sparkled on the bright paintwork of Duncan the little red tractor.

Stan, the farmer, looked up at the clear blue sky.

"Be all right for haymaking, anyway," he said. "But first we'll have to water the pigs."

He hitched the trailer onto Duncan's back hook. Then he lifted the water tank onto the trailer and filled it up with fresh, clean water.

"Right," said Stan. "Off we go."

The piglets were glad to see Duncan and raced up to him. They squealed, and pushed, and squirmed round his front wheels. They couldn't wait for Stan to fill the trough. They couldn't wait to slurp and snuffle in the nice, cold, ice cold water.

Stan cast an eye over the piglets.

"Seven, eight, nine –" he counted. "Hang on a minute. Where's Sidney?"

Stan looked round the mother pig. He looked behind the trough. He looked under Duncan and in the pigs' shed, and over the hedge. The piglet wasn't there.

"Sidney's got out of the field again," said Stan, scratching his head. "Hanged if I know how he does it. Only one thing for it, Duncan, we'll have to go and find him."

Stan drove Duncan back to the farmyard.

"Come on," he said. "Get a move on." He was in a hurry to find Sidney. But Duncan couldn't go any faster. He was suddenly feeling peculiar.

"Bit sluggish this morning," said Stan. "What's the matter with you?"

He backed Duncan up to the barn, and unhooked the trailer. Then he looked about for Sidney.

The hens didn't like Stan poking about in their favourite dark corners. They squawked, and flapped, and pecked crossly.

"All right, don't fuss," said Stan. "I'm only looking for Sidney."

Stan drove Duncan into Five Oaks field. The cows were resting under the trees in the shade, flicking at the flies with their tufty tails. A family of field mice twitched and trembled in the long grass. It was all quiet and peaceful. There was no sign of Sidney here.

"Sidney!" called Stan, just to make sure. But Sidney wasn't there. Duncan chugged over to the gate again. He felt strangely weak. Whatever *was* the matter with him?"

"You need an oil change, I expect," said Stan.

Duncan turned out of the field, and Stan gave a shout. There was Sidney trotting down the lane in front of them.

"Little scamp," said Stan. "Bet he wants to get down to the river. He'll wriggle under the gate into the sheep field. You mark my words."

Duncan set off after Sidney, but his engine started to cough.

"I know what's wrong with you," said Stan. "Spot of dirt in your fuel pipe."

He revved Duncan's engine up hard.

Whoosh! That was better. Duncan felt the power rush into him again. The speck of dirt had been blown right through. He was ready for action now.

Stan leaned out of Duncan's cab and looked down the lane. It was just as he'd thought. Sidney was squeezing under the gate, making for the river.

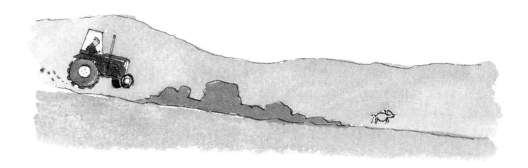

Duncan raced down the lane and turned into the sheep field.

"There he is!" shouted Stan. "Come on now, Duncan! We'll catch him down by the willow!"

Sidney ran straight across the field and into the water. It splashed round his trotters, and dripped off his tail. He bent his head for a long, cool drink.

Then, suddenly, Sidney saw the ducks.

"Oink! Oink!" he grunted and splashed after them. The ducks quacked and flapped with fright, and flew off into the wood.

Sidney looked round for something else to chase.

Duncan and Stan stopped on the river bank.

"Come on, Sidney," called Stan. "Time to go home."

Sidney took no notice. He was having fun. A minnow swam past his leg. It tickled! Sidney put his head down to look, and got a noseful of water.

"Achoo!"

Sidney sneezed, lost his balance, and rolled over into the water with a splash. He liked it! He stood up, and rolled over again. This was fun!

"Come on, will you!" shouted Stan. But Sidney still took no notice.

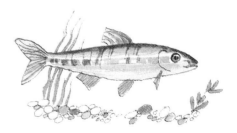

Stan shook his head, and patted Duncan's bonnet.

"We'll have to use a bit of cunning, Duncan old son," he said.

He put his hand in his pocket, and fetched out a carrot. Sidney put his head on one side and looked at it. He liked carrots.

Stan put the carrot on the ground. He hid behind Duncan's back wheel and waited.

Sidney lifted his wet shiny snout, and sniffed. He couldn't see Stan, but he could see the carrot, all juicy and crunchy, and sweet.

Sidney took one step towards the bank, and then he took another. Stan peeped out from behind the tractor.

"Here he comes now, Duncan," he whispered.

Sidney dashed forward, grabbed the carrot and started to run back into the water.

Stan jumped up, arms outstretched. Sidney squealed. Stan leaped forward, and fell with a squelch into the mud.

"Oh! You little devil!" shouted Stan, but he had caught Sidney, carrot and all.

Stan stood up and said a rude word. He was covered in mud, and so was the piglet he held in his arms. Sidney wriggled happily. He liked the mud. Stan looked down at him and laughed.

"You're a one, you are," he said.

Stan climbed back into Duncan's cab and Sidney leant his muddy snout on the bright red paintwork. Behind them, the swallows swooped over the water, catching insects for their babies.

Duncan bumped happily over the rough grass. He liked hearing Stan's cheerful whistle and Sidney's sleepy grunts. His engine was going fine now. He was firing on all cylinders, and ready for the haymaking.

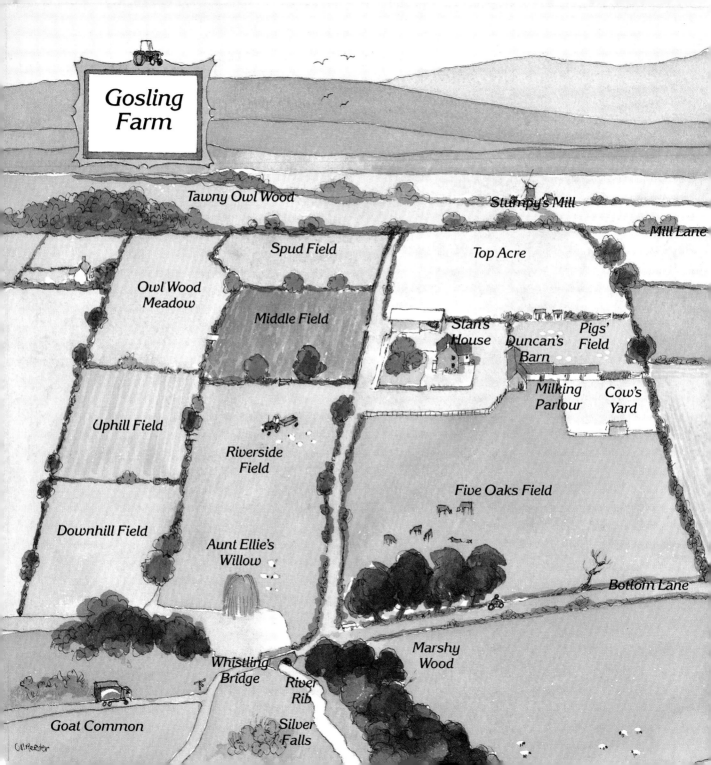

Gosling
Farm

Tawny Owl Wood

Stumpy's Mill

Mill Lane

Spud Field

Top Acre

Owl Wood
Meadow

Middle Field

Stan's
House

Duncan's
Barn

Pigs'
Field

Uphill Field

Riverside
Field

Milking
Parlour

Cow's
Yard

Five Oaks Field

Downhill Field

Aunt Ellie's
Willow

Bottom Lane

Whistling
Bridge

Marshy
Wood

River
Rib

Goat Common

Silver
Falls

Wrigglesworth

Beech Farm

Walter's
Garage

Heronwood Lake

River Dean